KT-555-999

The Disappearing Dinner

Fat Alphie and Charlie the Wimp

**Make friends with the greatest
alley cats in town!**

Be sure to read:

Fat Alphie in Love

... and lots, lots more!

The Disappearing Dinner

Margaret Ryan
illustrated by Jacqueline East

■SCHOLASTIC

For Joyce and Jim and Sam – with love M.R.

Scholastic Children's Books,
Commonwealth House, 1-19 New Oxford Street,
London, WC1A 1NU, UK
a division of Scholastic Ltd
London ~ New York ~ Toronto ~ Sydney ~ Auckland
Mexico City ~ New Delhi ~ Hong Kong

First published by Scholastic Ltd, 2002

Text copyright © Margaret Ryan, 2002
Illustrations copyright © Jacqueline East, 2002

ISBN 0 439 99460 8

All rights reserved

Printed and bound by Oriental Press, Dubai, UAE

10 9 8 7 6 5 4 3 2 1

The rights of Margaret Ryan and Jacqueline East to be identified as the author and illustrator of this work respectively have been asserted by them in accordance with the Copyright, Designs and Patents Act, 1988.

This book is sold subject to the condition that it shall not, by way of trade or otherwise, be lent, resold, hired out, or otherwise circulated without the publisher's prior consent in any form of binding or cover other than that in which it is published and without a similar condition, including this condition, being imposed upon the subsequent purchaser.

Chapter One

It was night time in Little Yowling.

The big humans were asleep and snoring.

The little humans were asleep and dreaming.

But the cats were awake and hungry.

Millie the Mouser
sat by a mouse hole,
waiting to pounce.
One-eared Tom
chased Clever Claws,
who had found a doughnut.

And, at number three Wheelie Bin Avenue,
Fat Alphie was getting
ready to go out
for dinner.

Fat Alphie
loved dinner,

and lunch,

and breakfast.

And he never
forgot elevenses or afternoon tea.

He washed his paws,
cleaned his ears and
nibbled his tail.

"Oi," yelled his friend, Charlie the Wimp,
"that's my tail you're nibbling."

"Thank goodness for that," said Fat Alphie,
spitting it out. "It's such a skinny tail, for a
moment I thought I was losing weight."

"Fat chance, the amount you eat,"
muttered Charlie the Wimp.
But Fat Alphie wasn't listening.

"Come on," he said.
"Time to go to
Sid's Diner for
my tuna-fish
starter."

"Do we HAVE to?" moaned Charlie. "I'd rather stay home and watch the telly."

Fat Alphie strolled down the middle of Main Street. Charlie the Wimp stayed close behind him, hanging on to his tail.

When they got to Sid's Diner, Fat Alphie searched the top of the rubbish bin. But tonight there was only rubbish.

"I don't believe it," he cried, disappearing inside the bin. "Sid always leaves me a bit of tuna fish for my starter. He knows it's my favourite!"

Charlie the Wimp looked round anxiously. "This place is scary. Let's get out of here. I'm sure I saw a large ear disappearing round that corner."

But Fat Alphie wasn't listening.

"Someone has stolen my starter," he moaned, and his tummy rumbled.

Then he cheered up. "But there's still my main course," he said. "Let's go to McPheeline's, the butcher's, and get my steak."

"Do we HAVE to?" moaned Charlie. "I'd rather go home and play with my rubber duck."

Fat Alphie strolled down the middle of
Main Street. Charlie the Wimp stayed
close behind him, hanging
on to his leg.

When they got to McPheeline's, the
butcher's, Fat Alphie searched the top
of the rubbish bin. But tonight there
was only rubbish.

"I don't believe it," he cried, disappearing inside the bin. "Mr McPheeline always leaves me a bit of steak for my main course. He knows it's my favourite."

Charlie the Wimp looked round anxiously. "This place is very scary. Let's get out of here. I'm sure I saw a large whisker disappearing round that corner."

But Fat Alphie wasn't listening.

"Someone has stolen my main course," he moaned, and his tummy rumbled even louder.

Then he cheered up. "But there's still my pudding," he said. "Let's go to Kit Kat's Café and get my chocolate cake."

"Do we HAVE to?" moaned Charlie. "I'd rather go home and play with my jingly ball."

Fat Alphie strolled down the middle of
Main Street. Charlie the Wimp stayed close
beside him, hanging on to his ear.

When they got to Kit Kat's Café,
Fat Alphie searched the top of
the rubbish bin. But
tonight there was
only rubbish.

"I don't believe it," he cried, disappearing
into the bin. "Kit Kat always
leaves me some chocolate
cake for my pudding.
She knows it's
my favourite."

Charlie the Wimp looked round anxiously. "This place is very very scary. Let's get out of here. I'm sure I saw a large tail disappearing round the corner."

But Fat Alphie wasn't listening.

"Someone has stolen my pudding," he moaned. And his tummy rumbled so loudly that Charlie the Wimp jumped up into his arms in fright.

"I told you I saw a large ear and a whisker and a tail,"
he cried.

"And here's the rest of me," said a loud voice, and a very large cat came round the corner, licking chocolate cake from his lips. "Oh no," cried Charlie the Wimp. "It's Mugger Magee!"

Chapter Two

Mugger Magee smiled a terrible smile.

I'm as mean as can be
I'm the cat you seldom see
I'm light on my paws
I've the sharpest ever claws
And with a rumble from MY belly
I can turn your legs to jelly

"Mine are jelly already,"
cried Charlie the Wimp.

So were Fat Alphie's,
but he was hungry.
Hungry and angry.

"You stole my
dinner," he yelled at
Mugger Magee. "No
one steals my dinner and gets away with it.
Chase him out of town, Charlie. I'll be right
behind you."

But Charlie ran off
the other way
as fast as his
wobbly legs
would go.

"Wimpy! Wimpy!" called Mugger Magee.
"And you couldn't catch me, Fatso, if I was
standing still with my paws in wet cement!
Looks like I'll be eating all your dinners
from now on. Looks like you've just gone
on a diet."

Mugger Magee laughed and strolled off leaving Fat Alphie to take his rumbling tummy home.

Back at number three Wheelie Bin Avenue, Fat Alphie and Charlie the Wimp sat down to have a think.

"I think we should leave town," said Charlie the Wimp, "till Mugger Magee goes away. He's as mean as can be. He's the cat you seldom see…"

"Yes yes," said Fat Alphie. "He's just trying to scare you."

"He's succeeding," muttered Charlie the Wimp.

"Well, I'm not leaving town," said Fat Alphie. "We'll outsmart Mugger Magee. We'll get to the eating places before him."

"Do we HAVE to?" moaned Charlie the
Wimp. "I'd rather stay home and hide."
Fat Alphie's tummy rumbled in reply.

The next evening they set out for dinner earlier than usual, but dinner was gone.

Not a crumb of cake,

not a nibble of steak,

not even a whiff of tuna fish was left.

Mugger Magee had beaten them to it.

And so it went on. Fat Alphie got thinner
and thinner. His ears drooped, his tail
drooped and his fine fur coat got baggy
and saggy.

"You're not looking well, Alphie," said
Millie the Mouser.

"Have you been ill, Alphie?" asked One-eared Tom.

"Off your food, Alphie?" asked Clever Claws.

"Did you notice," sobbed
Fat Alphie to
Charlie the
Wimp. "All
the other cats
just called me
Alphie. Not one

of them called me by my proper name.
I'm not Fat Alphie any more!"

Then he dried his eyes. "This can't go on.
We must do something
about Mugger
Magee."

"We!" gasped Charlie the Wimp. "Do you mean we, as in you and me?"

"Of course," said Fat Alphie. "But don't worry, I have a plan."

"That's what worries me," worried Charlie. But Fat Alphie wasn't listening.

"Do you remember last year's pantomime…"

☙ Chapter Three ❧

Very, very early next day Fat Alphie and
Charlie the Wimp hid behind Sid's Diner.

They waited and waited and waited.

"I don't like this," muttered Charlie the
Wimp, for the umpteenth time. "The sun's
gone down now, Mugger Magee will be
here soon. My knees are knocking, my teeth
are chattering and I'm shaking all over."

"Shush," said Fat Alphie.
"I think he's
coming."

Mugger Magee swaggered round the corner.
He was smiling and talking to himself.

I'm as mean as can be
I'm the cat you
seldom see...

He searched the rubbish bin behind Sid's
Diner, and had almost found the tuna fish,
when there was a loud MIAOW...

He looked round and just caught sight of a very large ear disappearing round the corner.

"Oh," he said. "What a very large ear. It must belong to a very large cat. Larger than me … perhaps I'll skip my starter tonight."

And he left without eating the tuna and
headed for McPheeline's, the butcher's.

Mugger Magee slid round the corner.
He was whispering to himself...

I'm light on my paws
I've the sharpest ever claws...

He searched the rubbish bin behind McPheeline's, the butcher's, and had almost found the steak when there was a very loud…

MIAOW…

He looked round and just caught sight of
a very wide whisker disappearing
round the corner.

"Oh," he said.
"What a
very wide
whisker. It
must belong
to a very wide
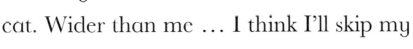
cat. Wider than me … I think I'll skip my
main course tonight."

And he left without eating the steak and headed for Kit Kat's Café.

At the top of Main Street Mugger Magee peered round the corner. He was muttering to himself...

And with a rumble from MY belly
I can turn your legs to jelly.

He searched the rubbish bin behind Kit Kat's Café and had almost found the chocolate cake when there was an ear-splitting...

MIAOW...

He looked round and caught sight of a
very long tail.

"What a very long tail," he whispered.
"It must belong
to a very long
cat. Longer
than me."

At that moment, a giant paw with giant claws came round the corner.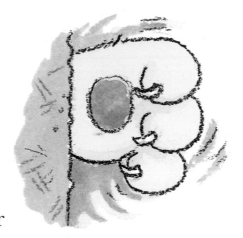

"It's a giant cat," whimpered Mugger Magee. "Larger, wider and longer than me. YIKES! I'm out of here. Right now!"

And he ran off as fast as he could.

Just in time, as a giant cat came round the corner. It had Fat Alphie's face and Charlie the Wimp's feet.

"We did it! We did it!" cried Fat Alphie. "We ran Mugger Magee out of town. Good thing we still had our Puss in Boots costume from the pantomime."

Charlie the Wimp peered out from the middle of the costume.

"I'm tired out," he moaned. "Next time you get a brilliant idea I want to stand on your shoulders."

"Oh stop moaning, Charlie," grinned Fat Alphie, jumping down. "Come on, it's dinner-time. Let's eat!"